CHRISTMAS MOUSE

Written and illustrated by Anne Mortimer

KATHERINE TEGEN BOOKS
An Imprint of HarperCollins Publishers

Also by Anne Mortimer

Bunny's Easter Egg
Pumpkin Cat

Katherine Tegen Books is an imprint of HarperCollins Publishers.
Christmas Mouse
Copyright © 2013 by Anne Mortimer
All rights reserved. Manufactured in China.
No part of this book may be used or reproduced in any manner whatsoever without
written permission except in the case of brief quotations embodied in critical articles
and reviews. For information address HarperCollins Children's Books, a division of
HarperCollins Publishers, 10 East 53rd Street, New York, NY 10022.
www.harpercollinschildrens.com

Library of Congress Cataloging-in-Publication Data is available.
ISBN 978-0-06-208928-1

The artist used watercolor on Arches hot press
watercolor paper to create the illustrations for this book.
Typography by Rachel Zegar
13 14 15 16 17   SCP   10 9 8 7 6 5 4 3 2 1
❖
First Edition

For Skye
Love,
Great Auntie Anne

Christmas Day is nearly here,
There's magic in the air,
Mouse is hanging festive lights
And holly on the stairs.

Pitter-patter up the tree
To hang some Christmas balls,

Pitter-patter down again,
Be careful not to fall!

Presents piled beneath the tree
Wrapped up for Christmas Day,

Leave one for a special friend
And quietly slip away.

Snowflakes softly falling down
And Robin's come to call.
"Would you like some gingerbread?
There's plenty for us all."

Pecan pie and sugared sweets,
Nibbles of nuts and cheese—
These are Mouse's favorite treats.
"Ice cream, Mouse?" "Yes, please!"

Pile the logs beside the fire,
Hang the paper chains.
Shall we light the candles, Mouse,
And what about some games?

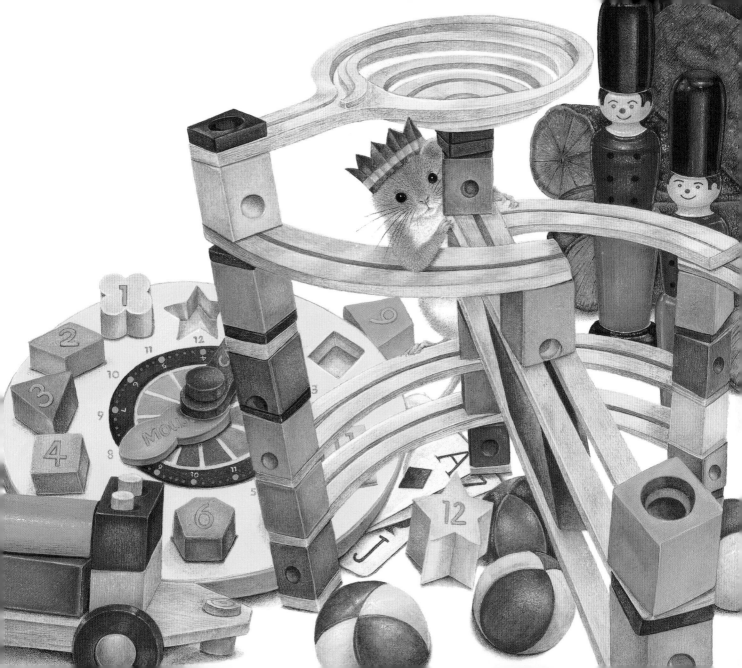

Carols sung beside the fire
With friends all gathered round,

Time to hang your stocking up
Before you snuggle down.

Starry, starry silent night,
Snow is lying deep,
Sleigh bells jingle high above,
Our friend is fast asleep.

Reindeer hooves upon the roof,
Santa Claus is due,

Make a wish, a Christmas wish,
Believe it will come true.

MERRY CHRISTMAS, EVERYONE!